is the bestselling author of the *Kidd* series, as well as other fiction for children and teenagers. She used to write for magazines *J17* and *Sugar*. Karen lives in London with her husband, small daughter and one fat cat.

Lydia Monks

won the Smarties Prize for *I Wish I Were a Dog*. She has illustrated many poetry, novelty and picture books for children, including *Little Big Mouth* for Walker Books. Lydia lives in Sheffield with her husband and daughter.

For Freya and her fabulously Fee-ish curls

KMcC

For Isabella

LM

This is a work of fiction. Names, characters, places and incidents are either the product of the author's imagination or, if real, are used fictitiously. All statements, activities, stunts, descriptions, information and material of any other kind contained herein are included for entertainment purposes only and should not be relied on for accuracy or replicated as they may result in injury.

First published 2008 by Walker Book Ltd
87 Vauxhall Walk, London SE11 5HJ

2 4 6 8 10 9 7 5 3 1

This book has been typeset in Granjon

Printed and bound in Great Britain by
Creative Print and Design (Wales), Ebbw Vale

British Library Cataloguing in Publication Data:
a catalogue record for this book is available from the British Library

ISBN 978-1-4063-1188-4

www.walkerbooks.co.uk

KAREN McCOMBIE • LYDIA MONKS

Me and the School (un) Fair

Welcome to my world
Me (Indie)
Ed
Mum
Dibbles
Carlsberg
George
Kenneth
Fish
Smudge
Nightingale

Soph & Fee
Simon Green
Mr Ioannou
Dad
Fiona
Miss Levy
Dylan
Caitlin

1

A whole lot of ooooooohhhhh-ing...

The school trampoline **ate** me last Thursday.

Thursday is our PE day, and everyone is supposed to **love** the trampoline, but I don't and the trampoline doesn't love me, which is why it **swallowed** my leg.

"Higher, Indie!" Miss Levy had called out, as I bounced, bounced, bounced in a weedy kind of way.

"Come on – let's see some energy.

Watched by my best friends Soph and Fee, as well as everyone else in my class, I really gave it my best shot.

I concentrated on thinking about my dog Dibbles, and how high he can jump when he's trying to steal food off the kitchen table and thinks you're not looking. (Trust me, it's very impressive for a short-legged, blob-shaped dog.)

If a non-athletic animal like Dibbles could do excellent leaping, then I guessed a reasonably fit ten-year-old girl called Indie could too.

But the trouble was, I concentrated so hard on thinking about Dibbles that I accidentally

bounced, bounced, bounced, bounced

sideways – and my left leg went **whooshing** down into the gap between the stretchy trampoline mesh and the metal frame.

And there I was, with one leg dangling down, my bottom balanced on a springy, rubbery rope. The other leg was bent up, so that my knee was by my ear.

Surprise, surprise, everyone laughed at me (even Soph and Fee, though they promised me afterwards that they'd tried incredibly hard not to).

You know, PE had never exactly been my favourite lesson before that happened. I just don't see the point of running or jumping for no reason, though I **love** running and jumping with all my dogs in the park. And climbing ropes and bars is rubbish compared with scrambling up trees with my step-brother Dylan.

Of course, ever since Thursday – what with the laughing and teasing and stuff – I'd decided that PE was absolutely and definitely my least favourite lesson in the entire **cosmiverse** and **beyond.**

And now? Well, now it was first thing Monday morning and time for assembly. I was sitting cross-legged on the floor of the school hall, scowling out of the window at the gym building right across the playground.

I wished I could wiggle my little finger and magic the whole building – especially the trampoline – away.

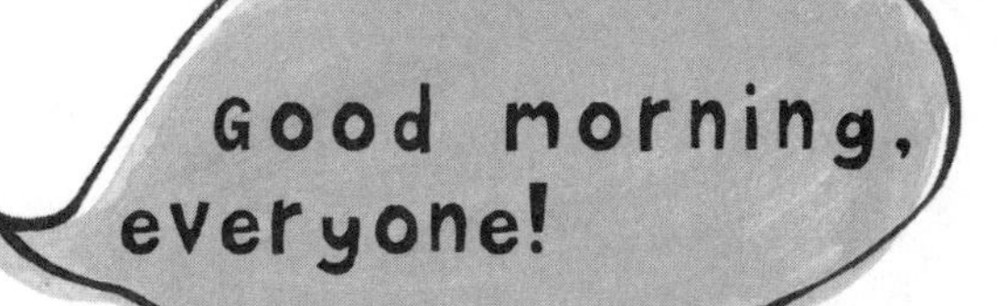

boomed Mr Ioannou, our head teacher, who was standing up on the stage at the far end of the hall.

"Good morning, Mr Ioannou," mumbled lots of not-quite-awake, Monday-morning voices.

"The first piece of news today is that there's a bad tummy bug going around school, so can everyone be on the look-out for the telltale signs of..."

Normally, I quite liked assembly. At the end of each one, Mr Ioannou would always hand out one of his

certificates to some lucky someone, and I always held my breath, hoping that one day, that lucky someone would be me. It made me tingle to think of stomping up to the stage to collect one, with the whole school clapping for me...

But today, I couldn't really concentrate on what Mr Ioannou was saying; I still had mild rubber burns on the back of my left thigh from the trampoline accident, which meant I had to sit at a slightly funny angle, just so it wouldn't hurt too much.

Then my attention was caught by someone making a funny noise.

It was me, actually.

"Ooooooooohhhhh..."

That wasn't a "**whee!**" sort of ooooooooohhhhh, by the way, it was more of a moany, groany ooooooooohhhhh.

And I was ooooooooohhhhh-ing because I'd just realized my leg had gone to sleep, thanks to sitting at that slightly funny angle.

I really wanted to unravel my leg and stretch it out, but the rule in school assembly is that you must sit still and quietly, all squished in tight rows like sardines (only without the slimy oil stuff).

The rows were so tight that I was in a best-friend sandwich, with my right knee jammed up against Soph's, and my left knee jammed up against Fee's.

Sitting directly in front of me was Simon Green. He was so close that I could have put my arms around him and given him a **big hug** – but you wouldn't want to do that with Simon Green, as he is as lovable as a germ.

"Oooooooooohhhhh!"

"Are you OK, Indie?" Fee whispered.

"Noooooooooohhhhh!" I moaned and groaned softly, rubbing at my leg as it went steadily dead.

"Is it cramp?" asked Soph, all concerned.

"No – it's just gone all … numb!"

"Uh-oh," mumbled Fee. "You know what *that* means…"

Uh-oh, no, I didn't know what that meant.

I couldn't think straight, 'cause of the funny numb feeling and the fact that I'd just felt a laser beam shooting our way.

Miss Levy, our teacher, was perched on a chair at the end of our row, and was glowering directly at me and my friends. Those wide eyes and arched eyebrows; they were Miss Levy's secret code for "Indie, Soph and Fee – whatever you're doing and saying, **DON'T!!**"

I didn't dare utter another mutter, and

neither did Soph or Fee. The only one doing any talking was Mr Ioannou, but being the Head, he was allowed.

"Now on to our next bit of news," Mr Ioannou continued. "The school has decided to hold a fair in two weeks' time—"

...I suddenly thought to myself (in a "**whee!**" kind of way). I liked school fairs. I liked them a lot. I liked the face-painting and the bouncy castles (a much more fun way to bounce than leg-eating trampolines). I liked the music and the tombolas and the mountains of home-made cakes to buy (and eat, eat, eat).

"—and this particular fair will be a fundraiser for our gym."

What?!

"We hope to replace lots of past-their-best pieces of equipment, and maybe even get ourselves a brand-new—"

Don't say it... I whispered in my head.

"—trampoline!"

"**Yay!**" chorused heaps of kids all around me.

"Boo!" I mumbled quietly, as I tried to wriggle myself into a slightly more comfortable position on the hard wooden floor.

At the same time, under cover of all the yay!-ing, Fee quickly tried to finish what she was saying to me before Miss Levy's Glower of Doom.

"Indie,watch out: you'll get that creepy pins-and-needles feeling the minute you try to move!"

Help - too late!

I'd only had room to move about an eighth of a centimetre, but it was enough to start a chain reaction of tiny "ooooooohhhhh!"s, with a few strangled "aaaaaaaaahhhhh!!"s thrown in. It felt like my leg was being bitten and tickled by a colony of ants.

"We will, of course, need a theme for our fair," Mr Ioannou boomed on, unaware of me wriggling and squiggling, just out of sight behind Simon Green. "And I thought we could make it into a competition, with all of you children trying to come up with—"

"Miss Levy!! Miss Levy!! Indie Kidd's gone MAD!!" yelped Simon Green, turning round to see what was going on.

The Glower of Doom fixed on me again, along with the eyes of every single person in the school hall.

Great.

Now I was in trouble, and that was *so* unfair.

Just like being eaten by a trampoline wasn't fair, or getting pins and needles, or sitting behind telltale Simon Green.

In fact, *everything* was unfair.

Even the School Fair – raising money for a new, killer trampoline – was *completely* unfair...!

2

The not-great ideas list

Everyone is good at something.

My friend Soph is good at Irish dancing (where your legs dance but your top half doesn't).

My other friend Fee is good at knowing long words, like "collywobbles" (which means either being very nervous or a type of jelly; I can't remember which).

My mum is the manager of the *Paws For Thought* Animal Rescue Centre and is good at looking after sick and homeless animals. (Just last night, she got called out to help capture a stray goat that had been spotted eating grass on a busy roundabout.)

My dad is good at taking wedding photos. (Though his ideas are a bit freaky: last Saturday he had a bride and groom bouncing on pogo sticks to symbolize jumping for joy...)

My step-mum Fiona is good at cooking (she writes recipes for the local newspaper), and my nine-year-old step-brother Dylan is good at being clever (but very, very bad at common sense).

And me? Well, I'm good at not staying grumpy for long, especially when there's something **fun** (like a competition) to think about. Especially if it means that I'll get one of Mr Ioannou's **"You Did Well!"** certificates in assembly if I win!

"Well, hello, girls!" said my old lady neighbour, Mrs O'Neill, appearing from behind her ultra-neat garden hedge, and snip-snipping at the edges of leaves with a tiny pair of nail scissors.

I jumped, and nearly dropped my dog Kenneth's lead **AND** the notepad I'd been scribbling in.

"Hello, Mrs O'Neill," I said back, at exactly the same time as Caitlin, who is…

A our lodger,

B good at playing the didgeridoo, and

C my childminder (she'd just picked me up from school that Tuesday afternoon).

Mrs O'Neill seemed pleased to see us, but not so keen to see our dogs.

Well, it wasn't so much Kenneth the Scottie dog, or George the greyhound, but Dibbles the daft dog.

Back when Dibbles was stuck in Mum's Rescue Centre and no one seemed interested in giving him a new home, I'd tried to matchmake him with Mrs O'Neill. But the afternoon when he went for a trial visit, he ate an unopened bag of toffees, a copy of the *Radio Times*, and a fruit basket that Mrs O'Neill had made out of lolly sticks.

That's when he ended up coming to live with us.

Mrs O'Neill did have a pet now, though. He was a budgie, and his name was Archie. I could just make him out, perched on his, er, perch in Mrs O'Neill's living-room window.

"You look very busy with that notebook, India!" said Mrs O'Neill, using my whole name, which no one usually does unless they're cross with me.

(By the way, Miss Levy wasn't cross with me yesterday, not once she realized I had a dead leg and wasn't just mucking about. She made me hop round the class to get the blood flowing properly again. She even got the whole class to do it too so I wouldn't feel silly.)

"And what might you be scribbling so carefully in there?" Mrs O'Neill carried on, pointing her tiny nail scissors at me.

"She was just writing down something I came up with!" Caitlin butted in, looking suddenly like a human maypole, **spinning** around with Dibbles and George and their leads, as they did circular **sniffing** duty.

"There's a competition to decide what the theme of our School Fair will be," I explained. "The winner will get a certificate from the head teacher."

Mrs O'Neill made an interested face. Though nothing on my list of ideas so far was that interesting.

So far, the themes I'd scribbled down were:

No one I loved seemed to have figured out that the theme of school fairs had to be something that wouldn't look stupid painted next to a sign that said "Food Stall" (I mean, bugs next to that?), or "Face-Painting" (a Neanderthal man?), or "Toilets this way" (a giant muffin?).

"And are you looking for more ideas, India?" asked Mrs O'Neill.

"Of course!" I said, encouragingly. After all, Mrs O'Neill was maybe 60 or 87 or 91, and had a lot of life experience. Maybe she would come up with an **amazing idea**.

"What about a theme of ... budgies!"

or maybe not.

"Hmm, that's ... good!" I lied, writing it down on the growing list of not-great ideas. "Got to get home now – give the pets their tea!"

As I smiled and waved and wandered off from Mrs O'Neill, I suddenly had the urge to phone Mum at work. She'd been so busy with goats on roundabouts and other animal emergencies that I hadn't talked to her yet about the competition. Maybe she might give me a sensible suggestion.

"Mum?" I said into my mobile, as Caitlin and I stumbled through the garden gate in a girl'n'dog jumble.

"Uh... Hi, Indie, honey!" Mum answered, sounding distracted.

"Listen, can you help me think of a theme for my School Fair?"

"Honey, I can't talk right now – I've got a parrot the size of a dodo sitting on my shoulder and I'm trying to manoeuvre him into a cage before he pecks some—owww!"

A dodo.

Some dodo-shaped thoughts suddenly flapped into my head.

I mean, you couldn't exactly have a theme of extinct animals (too odd), but maybe there was something I could do involving endangered animals?

Suddenly, I had it!

The School Fair could have an **eco** theme, with games like "Pin the Tail on the Endangered Lion-Tailed Macaque"!

My heart raced with excitement, even as I heard Mum owwwing some more in the background.

Yay! for the School Fair, and the winner of the choose-a-theme competition! (Who could be *me*, fingers crossed...!)

The flippety-flappety eco-map

Chuck-a-Sponge-at-a-Teacher Using recycled water.

Hit-the-Standby-Button Using coconuts painted red, under a gazebo made to look like a giant TV screen.

Plastic-Bag Modelling Turn these environmentally unfriendly bags into art!

The Guess-How-Many-are-Left-in-the-Wild Stall With prizes if you guess stuff like there're only 150 Golden Lion Tamarin monkeys left in the rainforests of South America.

A Bouncy Rainforest i.e. an inflatable bouncy castle covered with ivy chopped down from the side of the school wall.

All this and more was there for all to see (especially Mr Ioannou) on my sprawling eco-map of the school playground.

"You can't loosh," Dylan had said yesterday evening.

He'd come to mine for tea, and to help me with my competition entry.

"**What?!**" I'd frowned at him.

As far as I could remember, I'd never, ever "looshed" in my whole life, whatever that was.

Dylan chewed manically, finishing off the last bit of his post-tea snack sandwich. He looked like he was doing an impression of a beaver, fast-forwarded at high speed.

Then he **gulped**.

"I said, you can't lose," Dylan repeated, only speaking in English this time, and not gobbledegook. (Fee taught me that word. Good, isn't it?)

"Well, technically, I *can* lose,' I pointed out.

"No you can't – it's too good!"

My entry, with Dylan's excellent assistance, *was* very, very good. Dylan's drawing of the Northern Bald Ibis was especially good (I was planning a Hook-a-Northern-Bald-Ibis game instead of Hook-a-Duck, since the Northern Bald Ibis is on the endangered list).

But the thing was, even if I thought the eco-map was very good, I didn't dare say it out loud, 'cause it would have sounded bigheaded – and it could put a jinx on my chances of winning the "**You Did Well!**" certificate.

"How are you going to do it?" Dylan asked, in that maddening way he has of avoiding the sense in sentences.

"Do what?"

"Get it to school!"

"Under my arm, of course!" I told him confidently.

"It's too big," said Dylan.

"No it's not!" I contradicted him, grabbing hold of the giant sheet of drawn-on cardboard and intending to stick it under my arm. "There!"

I was having to hold my arm extremely tightly against my side, just to keep the card in place, since it was several centimetres too long for my fingers to reach the edge.

"Looks uncomfortable," stated Dylan.

I wish he wouldn't state things sometimes. It can get a bit annoying – especially when he's right.

"Well it isn't!" I fibbed.

If I thought standing in my room with the too-big card eco-map wedged under my arm was bad, you should've seen me next day on the way to school.

Even though there was just the tiniest of breezes, Caitlin had to grab the eco-map off me before I got blown flapping into the path of a number 17 bus.

Coming into school – where there were no breezes – was a real relief.

It was Friday, and the closing date for all the entries. Mr Ioannou would be judging them over the weekend and would announce the winner at Monday assembly. **(Yesss!)**

And now it was a real relief to bump into Fee, so I didn't have to flippity-flap my way along the corridor to Mr Ioannou's office on my own.

"Hey, Indie – what's that?" asked Fee, pointing at my eco-map.

"My entry for the competition!" I told her, surprised that she didn't realize what it was, considering I'd been talking about it non-stop all week. But I guess she just hadn't expected anything quite so big. "Where's yours?"

"Here!" said Fee, holding up a small piece of paper torn out of her favourite Hello Kitty notepad.

On it were the words:

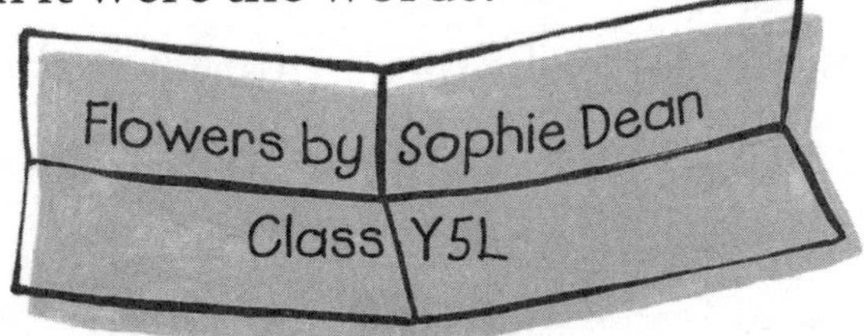

"I wasn't going to enter anything, but I thought of this on the way to school today and decided I might as well give it a go," Fee explained, folding her small piece of paper into an even smaller shape.

Now it looked like a book for a mouse.

"Hey, hi!" gasped Soph, running up from behind us. "What're you two doing?"

"Going to hand in our entries for the School Fair competition," I said.

Soph looked at my door-sized eco-map and then at Fee's **mouse-sized** book.

"Great! I'll come with you, 'cause I suddenly thought of something too!"

Soph pulled out a rolled-up sheet of lined paper and unrolled it like a scroll. She'd written:

Hawayan beach party!!!
By Sophie Musyoka. Y5L

"You don't spell it like that, Soph; it's H-A-W-A-I-I-A-N," said Fee.

Soph frowned at Fee as we walked along towards Mr Ioannou's office. "Sounds like way too many 'A's and 'I's to me! Are you sure?"

"'Course I'm sure!" said Fee, offended that anyone would question her excellent spelling skills.

(Mind you, I sometimes wondered if Fee ever made up words and how to spell them, knowing that Soph and I wouldn't have a clue. I mean, "flibbertigibbet" can't be a real word, can it? It sounds like a small, fat bird in a tutu, to me.)

Soph suddenly looked worried. "D'you think they'll disqualify my entry for bad spelling?" she asked in a mildly panicked voice.

"Maybe," said Fee, with the told-you-so shrug of a person who can spell well.

"What do you think, Indie?" Soph stared at me, hoping I'd make her feel better.

"Course not!" I told her, not believing either of the two words I'd just said.

Mr Ioannou was always going on about the importance of reading and writing and spelling and stuff.

Maybe he would disqualify Soph's entry, which would be a shame, 'cause if *my* entry didn't win, then I'd love to go to a Hawayan/Hawaiian beach party!

"Oh!" said Fee, as we turned the corner and found ourselves in the waiting area outside Mr Ioannou's office.

"Oh!" said Soph, turning to look at my giant-sized eco-map.

"Oh!" said little old me, once I spotted the shoe-box sitting on a chair in the waiting area.

It had a small slit cut in the top, and a notice taped to the back of the chair that read, "Please put your competition entries here".

"Um… Oh, well! Here goes!" Fee said awkwardly, popping her **mouse-sized** entry in the slot.

Pah.

I had as much chance of posting my entry as Dibbles had of winning a Handsome and Clever Dog competition. Which meant I had no chance of walking up onto the stage to collect a "**You Did Well!**" certificate with the whole school clapping for me.

This School Fair was turning out to be pretty unfair after all…

4

A fretty kind of mood

Monday.

School Assembly.

There was a lot of shuffling going on as everyone filed into the hall. I reckoned it was because there was more space than usual down at the front – half the Reception and Year 1 kids were off with the tummy-bug thing Mr Ioannou was going on about last week.

'Cause of all the noise and shuffling, maybe I had one more second to pester Miss Levy...

"Excuse me, Miss Levy, but are you sure?"

"I'm a hundred per cent sure, Indie!"

I looked pleadingly at Miss Levy, wishing she would say something that was even more reassuring than a hundred per cent.

Perhaps if she said she was really, truly, absolutely, cross-her-heart-and-hope-to-die a hundred per cent sure that Mr Ioannou had got my entry, then I could relax.

I mean, she'd been lovely to me on Friday, when she'd spotted me all hunched over my maths workbook. I think she could tell I wasn't really concentrating on it by the fact that it was upside-down and tears were sploshing onto it from the end of my nose.

When I explained about stuffing my eco-map behind the chair with the shoe-box on it (and being in a panic that a cleaner might think it was rubbish), Miss Levy promised me that she'd check with Mr Ioannou at breaktime.

"Mr Ioannou says he got it," she'd told me back in class, after I'd spent the entire break eating my crunchy muesli bar with my fingers crossed. **(Tricky.)**

"Definitely?" I'd checked with her.

"Definitely," she'd nodded back.

Then I'd felt better for a while. Well, till I went for lunch at Dad's on Sunday.

"Maybe your head teacher *didn't* get it, but told Miss Levy that he *did*!" Dylan had said to me, over third helpings of my step-mum Fiona's chocolate custard cheesecake.

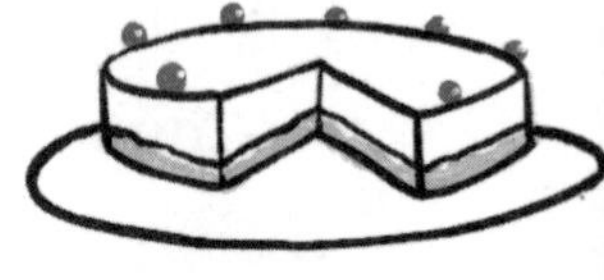

"Why would he do that?" I asked Dylan, feeling a knot tighten in my chocolate custard cheesecake-stuffed stomach.

"'Cause grown-ups lie all the time."

"**No we don't, Dylan!!**" my dad said, completely stunned.

"Oh, yeah? Well, how about Santa Claus and the Tooth Fairy and the Easter Bunny and 'No, your goldfish didn't die – I just gave him away to live with someone else'?"

Dad gulped.

"Maybe your head teacher said he got your entry just to make you feel better," Dylan carried on, "and you've got no way of knowing if that's true or not, 'cause he's a grown-up and can say whatever he wants!"

Dad looked like he was trying to come up with something very reassuring, but his mind seemed to be jammed.

So I'd come home in a **fretty** kind of mood, and gone to sleep in a **fretty** kind of mood, and turned up at school today in a **fretty** kind of mood.

Which is why I was bugging Miss Levy with "Are you sure?" questions again.

"Now, Class Y5L – everyone settle down!!" Miss Levy ordered us.

I think it was her way of ignoring my pleading, puppy-dog eyes.

"Ooh, look!" Soph nudged me, as we folded our legs up.

I looked where she was looking.

"She must have broken it, then!" hissed Fee.

The "she" was Melanie McKay in Year 6. The "it" that she must have broken was her arm.

Melanie McKay was **famous** at our school for being the fastest across the monkey bars on the playframe.

But at afternoon break on Friday she could have won a prize for the most painful fall from the monkey bars ever.

Next thing she was being led off to the medical room by her teacher. But by the look of that bright red plaster cast on her arm, she'd ended up spending the rest of Friday at the hospital.

Shhhhhhhh!

Miss Levy shushed us all, just in time for Mr Ioannou to step up to the front of the stage.

"Good morning, everyone!" he boomed brightly.

"Good morning, Mr Ioannou..." we all mumbled.

"Well, I hope you all had a super weekend and are all ready to work very hard this week at—"

I know this is bad, but I think all everyone heard for the next five minutes was **"Blah, blah, blah"**. I mean, all anyone really wanted to hear was who'd won the "**You Did Well!**" certificate. Or maybe that was just me.

"And now on to the competition results...!"

All around, I could feel people wake up and start listening properly again. It was pretty amazing that I noticed, considering that my heart was pounding so hard I felt giddy.

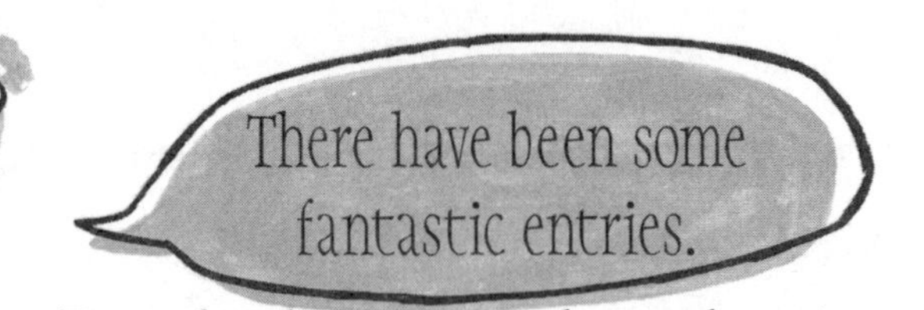

(People always say that when it comes to announcing winners of competitions. Nobody ever says, "All the entries were rubbish, so it was a doddle to pick a winner.")

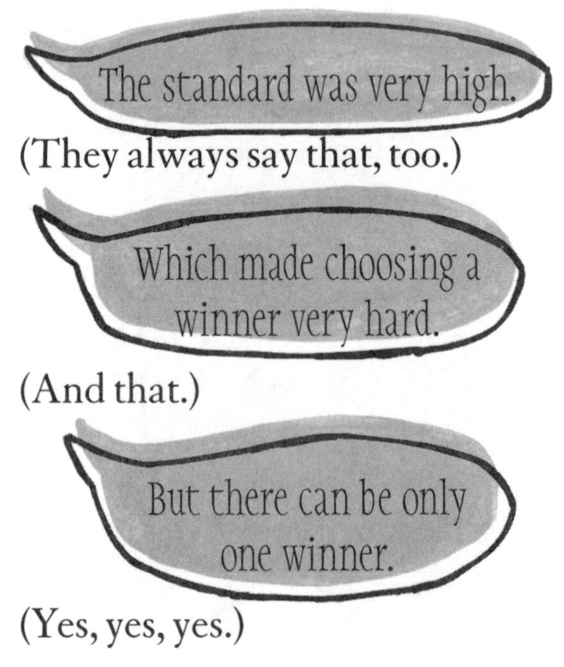

(They always say that, too.)

(And that.)

(Yes, yes, yes.)

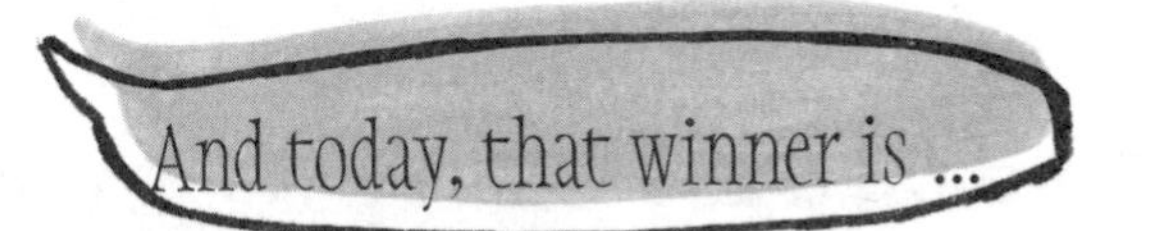

Someone somewhere started drumming fast on the floor with their hands. People started sniggering, and a teacher from Year 4 did a very cross "Shushh!" at someone I couldn't see.

I felt so nervous I worried that I might be a little bit sick.

I saw two arms go up in the air in a winning salute, one in a red plaster cast.

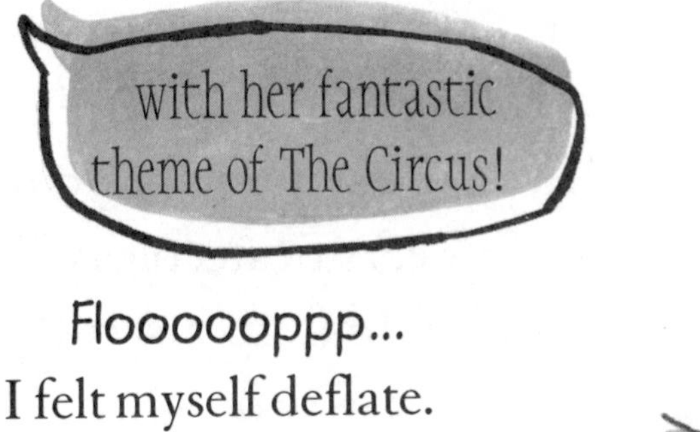

Flooooopppp...
I felt myself deflate.

The circus?! That was a … well, it wasn't a terrible idea, like Alien Bugs or Muffins or Budgies, but it was pretty dull.

Honestly, I wouldn't have minded not winning (much) if the theme had been so amazing it made my head – **ping** – with excitement.

Instead my head went "Hmmm…", as I tried to figure out *why* Melanie's entry had won.

Had Mr Ioannou run out of time to read through all the entries at the weekend? Had he just done eeny-meeny-miny-mo instead?

"Melanie! If you'd like to make your way up here for your certificate, please!" said Mr Ioannou, holding up a scruffy sheet of A4 with the word "Circus"

written on it in different-coloured inks. "And let's give her a big round of applause!"

BOO – should've been me, I thought meanly (but I couldn't help it).

And pah! – Dylan was right. My head teacher had probably never seen my eco-map after all. I bet it had been tidied away by a super-keen cleaner and was now in one of the school's mega-bins under a ton of leftover shepherd's pie.

"And as Melanie makes her way up, I'd just like to mention another excellent entry – by India Kidd. Where are you, India?"

I got violently nudged by elbows on either side of me (Soph and Fee were excited, I could tell).

Shaking ever so slightly, I stuck my hand up in the air.

"Ah, India," said Mr Ioannou, fixing his gaze on me. "Your ecology idea really was very well thought out and excellently presented!"

I felt a wibble of pride at the compliment, then a wobble of confusion.

How come – if my idea for a theme was so well thought out and excellently presented – Melanie McKay's kind-of-OK-ish circus theme had won?

As I lowered my hand, it dawned on me. 'Cause she'd broken her arm, **that's why!**

"He just felt bad for her 'cause she fell off the school monkey bars and hurt herself!" whispered Fee, reading my mind.

Huh! That was *so* unfair. I mean, why couldn't *I* have broken my arm?

Er, maybe I didn't quite mean that...

The invisibly excited Dylan

I am under strict instructions from both my mum and my dad that I should only ever use my mobile phone in emergencies.

This is because they worry that mobile-phone waves can melt children's brains. (Grown-ups' brains must be made of harder stuff.)

But today, I had to use it because there **WAS** a genuine emergency.

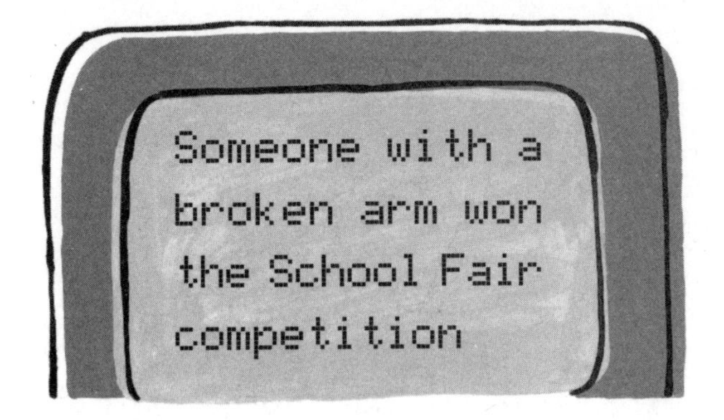

I texted Dylan during Monday lunch-hour.

(I figured that texting isn't near your head and so can't melt it. Though maybe it could melt your finger…?)

Dylan – who is also under strict instructions from my dad and *his* mum only to use his mobile in emergencies – texted me straight back. "That is very VERY bad news."

Mum's turn next for the **very**, **VERY** bad news.

"So sorry, Indie – know how hard you and Dylan worked on it," Mum replied. "But want to know something good? We have just had a chinchilla brought in to the Rescue Centre!"

Now here were three things I knew for sure about Dylan:

Ⓐ He wasn't allowed a pet, ever. (His mum was scared of all animals, not just the scary ones. Fiona would scream just as loud if she found a baby hamster in her house as if she found a panting, stomping rhinoceros.)

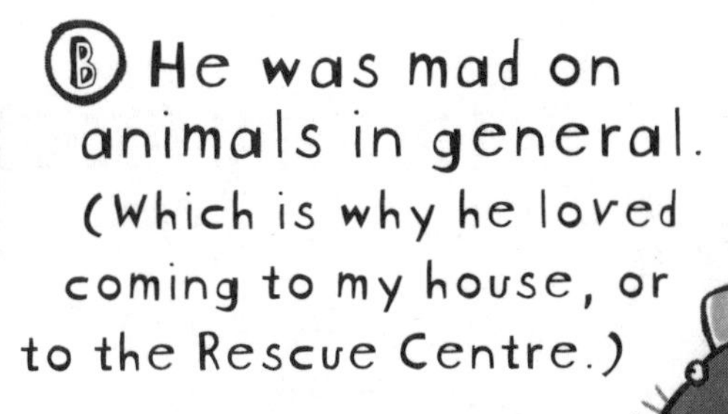

Ⓑ He was mad on animals in general. (Which is why he loved coming to my house, or to the Rescue Centre.)

Ⓒ He was mad on chinchillas in particular. (Even though he'd never met one.)

I texted Dylan the emergency good chinchilla news.

"Can I see it?" he texted back.

Quite a few texts later, and it was all sorted: Caitlin would take me to the Rescue Centre after school, and Fiona would drop Dylan off there.

Three hours later, we were sitting in the reception, waiting patiently for Mum. I was passing the time by inspecting my finger for any signs of text-related melt-iness.

"I'm very excited."

I looked at Dylan. Anyone who didn't know him would think he was the exact opposite of excited, 'cause he was sitting perfectly still and his face had a sort of blank expression on it.

I could see Rose the receptionist secretly staring at him over the top of her glasses. I think she was wondering if he was being sarcastic, but he wasn't.

"Do you want to know an interesting fact about chinchillas?" Dylan suddenly asked, to anyone who happened to be listening.

"**NO**," said Caitlin, flicking through her music magazine.

"**Yes!**" said me and Rose the receptionist.

"Well, chinchillas make funny noises, like barking and chirping and—"

Dylan didn't get any further, because Mum had just come through the swing door with a very round, shy-looking parrot attached to her shoulder. Its head was hunkered down, as if it wanted to pull it into its body, turtle-style.

Mum said to us all.

"That's not a chinchilla," said Dylan very definitely.

"Nope – this is Ed, and he's very nervous," said Mum, stroking the pudgy tummy of the parrot resting on her shoulder. "He comes everywhere round the centre with me at the moment – he won't go to anyone else."

Mum still had a plaster on her finger from the sharp peck that Ed the dodo-parrot had given her when he first arrived last week.

She'd decided to let him perch on her shoulder till he got braver. The only problem was, with all that weight, she was starting to walk a little lopsided.

"He's a bit fat," said Dylan bluntly – which is the way Dylan usually talks, unfortunately.

"His old owner fed him sausage and chips, which of course was very bad for him," Mum told Dylan. "He's on a strict diet of seeds and fruit now."

"Crauwkkk!" said Ed, which might have been parrot-speak for "Don't call me fat!" or "Ooh, I do miss those chips…".

"So, want to see the new goat?" Mum asked cheerfully, heading back to the swing door.

"What about the chinch—"

"It's on the way to the chinchilla, Dylan," Mum interrupted him with a smile.

We trotted after her – me, the invisibly excited Dylan, and Caitlin, her nose still buried in her magazine.

"And this is Nightingale," said Mum, walking us into the concrete dog (and goat) block.

"Why's it called Nightingale?" asked Dylan, staring at the black and white goat that stared right back at him.

"'Cause she was picked up on the Nightingale Corner roundabout," Mum told him.

"How did she get there?" Dylan asked.

Mum sighed a sigh that she often sighs when she's thinking about cruelty to animals. "Well, someone reported that they saw a man in a van deliberately dump her. It's a wonder she didn't get run over in the rush-hour traffic."

"You know, Nightingale's a bit of a long name," I butted in. "Maybe you could call her *NME* instead, since she's eating Caitlin's copy of the *NME*?"

"**What!!**" shrieked Caitlin, who hadn't noticed the nibbling going on in the bottom right-hand corner of her magazine.

It seemed like a good time to move on, straight to the small-mammal room, where a grapefruit-sized bundle of fur with ears was spiralling around a cage like a demented fluffy whirlwind.

"What's it doing?" I asked Mum.

"Carlsberg's just excited. He's hoping for a treat!"

Caitlin quickly folded up her magazine, in case chinchillas called Carlsberg were as keen on paper as goats called Nightingale.

"Carlsberg?" I frowned at Mum.

"The bloke who owned him named him after a kind of beer," said Mum, rolling her eyes. "We're going to have to think of a much nicer name than that. Do you want to feed him, Dylan?"

"Yes, please!" Dylan said breathlessly, as he watched Mum take a few raisins out of one of the many pockets in her khaki-green work trousers.

"Just give him one. They're his favourite thing ever, but too many and he'll get diarrhoea."

Ha! Like all the kids in Reception and Year 1...

At the mention of diarrhoea, Caitlin made a gagging noise and went over to lean on the wall on the far side of the room and read her music magazine in peace.

As quickly as it had spiralled, the furry grey bundle was now completely still, dark eyes wide and tiny paws clinging to the bars of the cage. Dylan offered the raisin … which was daintily taken and then nibbled in a nanosecond.

Then – as if he wanted to show us how happy he was – Carlsberg started **boinging** all over his cage, like a soft grey ball of fluff on springs.

"He is the cutest thing I've ever seen…" sighed a besotted Dylan.

"Not to his last owners," said Mum. "Because he's mostly nocturnal he annoyed them by squeaking at night."

"Crauwkkk!!"

Yikes – I quickly turned my head and followed the sound of flapping.

"**Help!!**"

"Wow, Caitlin! You are honoured! You're the only other person he's ever gone to in here!" Mum said in amazement.

Caitlin didn't seem very honoured. With Ed the parrot balancing on the top of her head, she looked more terrified and embarrassed. A terrified and embarrassed teenage perch.

But at that very moment, something hit me (a thought, not a thing, thank goodness). All of a sudden I decided to stop fretting over the unfairness of the School Fair.

'Cause animals being treated badly was **TRULY** unfair, and for me, meeting Ed, Nightingale and Carlsberg had suddenly helped put everything into … um … whatever that big word is that Fee knows. Y'know – when you decide what's important and what's not.

Still, I guess what was most important right now was helping untangle a pair of sharp claws from my childminder's head.

Crauwkkk…!!

6

A big hand for Indie...

"It's staring at me..."

"It's not staring at you, Indie!" Soph tried to reassure me.

But it was. I know when a trampoline is giving me dirty looks.

It was Tuesday afternoon, and we were in the school gym, where my class were painting some circus-y decorations on hardboard for the Fair this Saturday. The tea and cake stalls were going to be in here. **(Mmmmm...)**

Me and Soph, we were painting the red and white stripes of a circus tent, which was going to be the frame for the door of the gym.

"Indie, a trampoline can't stare at you," sighed Fee. "It's an inanimate object."

It's like that word I couldn't think of yesterday: "perspective". Fee sure does know an impressive number of words, she really does.

She is definitely not very artistic, though.

"Er, Fee... What's that supposed to be?" I asked, turning my head sideways, sort of hoping that might help me make out what exactly my friend had painted.

It didn't.

"It's an acrobat on the flying trapeze," explained Fee, pointing the end of her paintbrush at a black blob dangling off two streaky yellow lines.

I was glad she'd explained. I was just about to say it looked like a bee with all its yellow stripes unravelling, but I didn't know of too many bee circuses.

"Hey, look at that!" Soph interrupted, pointing at the end wall, where Miss Levy was fixing up a row of tumbling, juggling, goofing-around clowns.

They'd been done by the Year 6s this morning. The hardboard clown paintings had been stacked in a long line in the corridor when we'd come into the gym after lunch.

(I accidentally backed into one – a painting, not a Year 6 person – when Simon Green pushed past me. Luckily, that particular clown was still in one red-nosed, big-footed piece when I turned around to check him out.)

"**They look cool!**" I admitted, trying to be totally positive about the whole circus theme.

After all, the Fair would be fun, even if there was nothing eco about it. (Sniff.)

And looking around, I could see everyone was having such a good time chatting and giggling and getting stuff ready for it, that I could hardly stay grumpy about losing the competition.

"Ah! Simon!" Miss Levy suddenly called out, turning her head as if she was scanning around for help. "Could you come here and give me a hand, please?"

Simon Green seemed to find what she'd just said very, very funny, which it wasn't particularly. Who knows why? Perhaps just because – like I said – everyone was in a great mood. Or perhaps just because he was Simon Green and he was a **great big noodle.**

"Sorry, I can't give you a hand right now, Miss Levy!" he managed to snigger. "But I definitely think *Indie* could give you a hand!!"

Miss Levy narrowed her eyes at him, slightly irked. But as the clown painting she was trying to put up was tilting dangerously to one side, she didn't have time to hassle him.

"Indie?" she called out to me instead. "Can you help me hold this, please?"

"I'm coming!" I shouted back, hurrying over to her.

As I hurried, three things happened:

1) Simon Green and his mates burst out laughing.
(Huh?)

2) Simon Green shouted, "A big hand for Indie!!"
(Huh?!?)

3) Lots of people started clapping and laughing too.
(Huh?!?!?)

Just before I got to Miss Levy, I turned around to stare at everyone, trying to figure out what was going on.

I couldn't.

And in a few backward steps, I was by Miss Levy's side.

Good grief; Miss Levy was **giggling** too!

What *was* this?

"Um, Indie – I think you might have sat or leant on a wet painting," Miss Levy explained, pointing at... Oh, the shame!

She was pointing at my bottom.

I squizzled round to see what was wrong with it, and found myself staring down at a clown's giant, white-gloved hand.

Aargh!

It must have happened when Simon Green pushed past me in the corridor earlier. For the last hour, I'd thought everyone was giggling 'cause they were in a happy mood, but really it was because I had a stupid, great big painted hand on the bum of my best jeans.

Why me?

Humph... Maybe the trampoline had put a jinx on me – I told you it didn't like me.

Or maybe it was just another case of School Fair un-fairness...

The power of please

Bullying is a **very bad thing.**

But it's OK when the person you're bullying is your dad, and it's for a good 'cause.

"How much did you say they were?" asked Dad, keeping an eye on the road, since he was driving.

"Fifty pence," I told him, holding on tight to a white envelope stuffed full of School Fair raffle tickets.

"Can I go and see the chinchilla again?" Dylan asked, sitting beside me in the back of the car.

Dad and I both ignored him. Since he'd met Carlsberg the chinchilla yesterday, Dylan had become obsessed. He'd texted me nine times, e-mailed twice, and phoned the house once to chat to Mum about him. And since Dylan lived with Dad and Fiona, they'd probably heard about the cuteness of Carlsberg **non-stop.**

"Well, I'll buy ... ten tickets, then!" said Dad.

"**Ten! Only ten?**" I squeaked. "Dad – these raffle tickets are raising money for something very important!"

"I could go into the Rescue Centre when we drop Indie off after tea. I could just say hi really quickly to the chinchilla!" Dylan carried on, though no one was listening.

"Yes, Indie, but you said that the very important something was the gym, and you've never been very keen on the gym, have you!"

What Dad said was true, obviously. But I was keen on competitions. So even though I'd only just talked myself out of being disappointed about the School Fair theme thing, here I was again, hoping to win the next "**You Did Well!**" certificate from Mr Ioannou for selling the most raffle tickets.

(Please, please, please!)

"But that would be five pounds, Indie, which is quite a lot!" Dad pointed out.

"Did you know that chinchillas have sixteen hairs to one human hair, which is why they're so soft and furry and cute?" said Dylan, happily having a conversation with himself.

"Please, Dad, please buy some more. I really want to sell the most. Please, Dad!" I pleaded.

"Well, Indie, I think five pounds is en—"

"**PLEASE, PLEASE, PLEASE, PLEASE, PLEASE, PLEASE!!**"

Dylan looked at me, and seemed to realize I was onto something.

"Can I see the chinchilla when we drop Indie off? **PLEASE, PLEASE, PLEASE, PLEASE, PLEASE, PLEASE!!!!**"

Poor Dad. One pizza and milkshake tea at a café later, and we were on our way to the Rescue Centre.

Our avalanche of pleases had worked really well, and Dylan had been promised fifteen minutes of hanging out with Carlsberg, while Dad had agreed to buy **twenty pounds'** worth of raffle tickets!

The "**You Did Well!**" certificate was practically mine! Everyone would be cheering and clapping for me! (In a good way, not in a bad way, like when they were giggling at me having a clown's hand print on my bottom.)

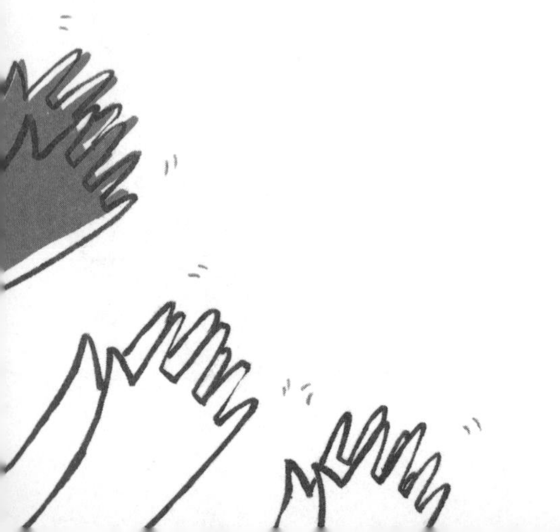

Over the next few days, I knew I could sell some tickets to neighbours like Mrs O'Neill. And here at the Rescue Centre, well, maybe Rose the receptionist and some of the nice vet nurses and kennel assistants would help me out and buy some too.

Especially if I tried to make my eyes go all cute and pleading, the way Dibbles does when he's hoping you'll spare a crisp for him from your packet of cheese'n'onion.

And of course Mum would—

"Oh! What's going on here?" said Dad suddenly, in a voice that was meant to sound calm but had an edge of panic to it.

And **whoosh** – I felt a wave of panic now too, since there were two fire engines parked outside the *Paws For Thought* Rescue Centre.

"Mum! And all the animals!!" I croaked unhappily.

"Carlsberg!!" Dylan mumbled in a wibbly-wobbly voice.

"It could just be a fire drill!" Dad tried to reassure us, as he quickly parked the car.

"With real smoke?" asked Dylan, his eyes drawing mine to the faint grey haze above the building.

Squish! of an envelope of tickets being shoved into my back pocket; **clunk!** of a seatbelt; **slam!** of a car door, and **thud, thud, thud!** of three pairs of running feet.

"Indie, it's all fine, it's all under control," Rose blurted out from behind the desk as soon as she saw us. "Your mum's through in the dog block, if you want to go straight—"

I was through before she could say the word, with Dylan and Dad right behind me, heading for the dog block at top speed.

Blam! went the dog-block door, and there was Mum, in deep conversation with a firefighter. She was holding Nightingale the goat by a lead, with Ed the parrot perched fatly on her shoulder, delicately tugging a bit of stray hay out of her blonde hair.

"**Mum!!**" I called out, relieved to see her looking alive and well and unsinged around the edges.

"Indie, honey!" she called out to me, at the same time giving a smile to Dylan and a wave to my dad.

"Better be off," the firefighter said, tapping his big yellow plastic hat.

Good. If he was off, that meant there were no life-threatening fires happening any more.

But what exactly had happened?

"Are any of the animals hurt?" I blurted out.

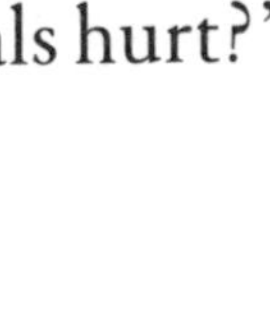

"No – no one and nothing is hurt," Mum assured me. "There was a small, electrical fire in the cat block, but it got put out very quickly. All the cats are fine, although they will have to eat their tea by candlelight tonight!"

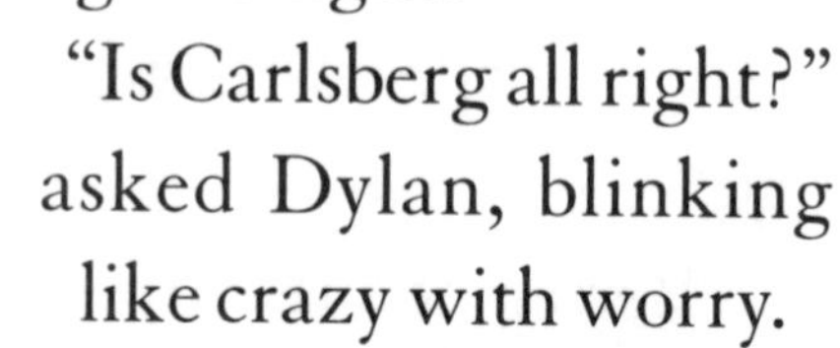

"Is Carlsberg all right?" asked Dylan, blinking like crazy with worry.

"Ah, Carlsberg…" Mum replied, in an **odd** kind of way.

"Is he all right?" asked Dad, putting his hands on Dylan's shoulders, in a comforting way, in case bad news was rumbling along at any moment.

"He's fine," Mum said quickly.

Phew…

"He just caused us a few problems. He escaped from his cage earlier, somehow got into the fusebox, and tried eating the cable."

"Why did he do that?" I asked.

"Well, maybe he thought it would taste of raisin?" suggested Dylan, staring earnestly at my mum.

"Perhaps..." Mum shrugged, which was quite hard to do with a hefty parrot on one shoulder.

"So Carlsberg caused the fire in the cat block?" I asked, double-checking that I understood what she was saying.

"**Yep!** Those dainty little hands of his seem to be good at picking locks on cages!"

"Chinchillas are famous for having very agile paws," Dylan chipped in with a slightly-too-late-to-be-useful fact.

"Will the damage be easy enough to fix?" Dad asked.

"The good news is that the fusebox and cable will be easy to fix. The bad news is that the firefighter told me that all the wiring in the cat block looks very out of date, and it's going to cost a lot to replace."

Uh-oh. The Rescue Centre never had very much money ever, so how would they manage now?

"Indie..."

I frowned at Dylan, sure he was about to come out with some dumb chinchilla fact when there was a hugely serious problem to think about.

"What?" I said, probably a bit impatiently.

"I think the goat has eaten your stuff."

Urgh...

A sad, useless corner of white envelope stuck out of Nightingale's mouth, as she happily chewed on sixty pounds' worth of School Fair raffle tickets.

Something told me I wouldn't be walking up onto the stage to collect that "**You Did Well!**" certificate from Mr Ioannou on Monday...

8

The Truly Fantastic Thing

A **thunderbolt** of inspiration hit me at two o'clock this morning.

(Actually, it was nine minutes past two, but saying "A thunderbolt of inspiration hit me at nine minutes past two o'clock this morning" doesn't sound so dramatic.)

After the close call at the Rescue Centre, I'd been having a mad, bad dream where all the animals were stuck in their cages in terrible danger, but then the water in the firefighters' hoses suddenly turned to showers of raffle tickets.

In my dream, Nightingale the goat kept getting in my way, trying to eat the tickets as they rained down.

I woke up with my orange duvet in a tangle (it looked like a cheese twist) and Kenneth my Scottie dog licking my face.

Flicking on the light, I sat for a second, waiting for my heart to stop racing. As it **thumpety-thumpety-thumped**, I gazed round at the menagerie (see, I know big words too!) dotted around my room. My three dogs were sprawled on, beside or in my bed (the big orange lump by my feet had to be Dibbles undercover).

Smudge the cat was curled up on the clothes I should've put in the laundry basket.

And of course there were the others.

Our fish (One, Two, Three, Four, Five, Five-and-a-half and Brian) would be **swooshing** around in their tank downstairs.

Carlsberg – who Mum had brought home from the rescue centre to keep an eye on – would be curled up in his temporary cage in our kitchen (unless he'd picked the lock and eaten through the gaffer tape holding the door closed).

Anyway, as I was looking at my pets and thinking about my pets, that's when the **thunderbolt** of inspiration struck.

And it struck like this...

First, I suddenly realized that recently I'd been whingeing on (and on) about how unfair stuff was, which made me sound as if I wasn't having any luck or something.

But actually, even if I *had* been pretty unlucky to be eaten by a trampoline, or beaten in a contest by a girl who'd broken her arm, I was one hundred per cent lucky to have all these **truly fantastic** pets, compared with lots of other kids.

And that's what made me think of a **Truly Fantastic Thing!** (It'll all make sense in a second, honest.)

Only I didn't know if my head teacher would think it was such a **Truly Fantastic Thing** (even once I'd explained how fantastic it was).

"Just knock!" Fee urged me, as we stood outside Mr Ioannou's office door at twelve o'clock the next day.

I think Fee wanted me to hurry up because…

"Maybe Mr Ioannou's gone for his lunch now!" I muttered, looking for a way out.

"He hasn't," whispered Soph, with her ear stuck against the door. "I can hear him in there... He's humming something... It's 'Can't Get You Out of My Head', by Kylie!"

It should have felt like a good omen, since it's one of my favourite songs too, but I still felt hugely nervous.

"Y'know, I should've just told Miss Levy my idea," I mumbled, in a chickening-out tone of voice. She'd been lovely to me this morning, telling me that the goat-chewed tickets weren't a problem – she'd explained that the office would just give me some more.

"Don't be silly, Indie: we talked about this," said Fee, sounding stern. "There's no time for messing about,'cause the Fair's only three days away. Now practise your big-eyed pleading expression again!"

I thought of Dibbles, and pulled a suitably cute and hopeful face.

"Good! Now knock on—"

Aaarrgghhh!!

The door flew open on its own!

We all froze – me with my Dibbles face – as Mr Ioannou gazed down at us all.

"And what can I do for you ladies?" he asked.

Uh-oh – I couldn't speak. I really was frozen. I couldn't get the words out at all, even when Soph and Fee nudged me hard from either side.

I heard Fee sigh, knowing that a golden opportunity to tell Mr Ioannou my **Truly Fantastic Thing** was passing by. Not to mention the chance to get a Mexican wrap before they ran out.

"Lots of children don't have pets!" Soph suddenly announced.

"Well, no, they don't," said Mr Ioannou, probably wondering what this was about, and wishing he'd stayed in his room humming Kylie hits.

"And it would be great if they got the chance to hang out with animals and pat them and stuff!" Soph added, not really making herself any clearer.

Still, she was doing better than me.

Mr Ioannou scratched his head, and tried again to understand what might be going on. "Mmm, that would be good, I suppose!"

"Exactly!" Fee dived in. "So Indie thought that maybe there could be a Petting Zoo at the School Fair on Saturday. Her mum could come with lots of the cute animals from the Rescue Centre she works at!"

Fee beamed at me, hoping I would carry on. But nope. I was like a human statue with a pathetically hopeful dog face stuck on.

"Oh!" said Mr Ioannou. "Well, that does sound quite—"

"It would be really good fun, and could raise lots of money for the gym, if you charged fifty pence to pat a goat or something," Fee carried on, realizing I was truly hopeless at explaining the **Truly Fantastic Thing**.

"And there was a fire at the Rescue Centre," Soph babbled, trying to help out. "And they can't afford to fix it up."

"Hold on; but the money made would have to go to the school gym," Mr Ioannou said dubiously. "It would be too complicated to have people donating to the school *and* the Rescue Centre..."

"Oh no!" Fee jumped in. "Indie just thought it would be good publicity. Maybe people would come along and find out more about the Rescue Centre, if they had fun at the Petting Zoo!"

"Hmm. Well, Indie, that sounds ... interesting," Mr Ioannou nodded at me, even though I hadn't said a word. "But I worry that it would be too hard to organize at such short notice, considering—"

Finally I found my voice.

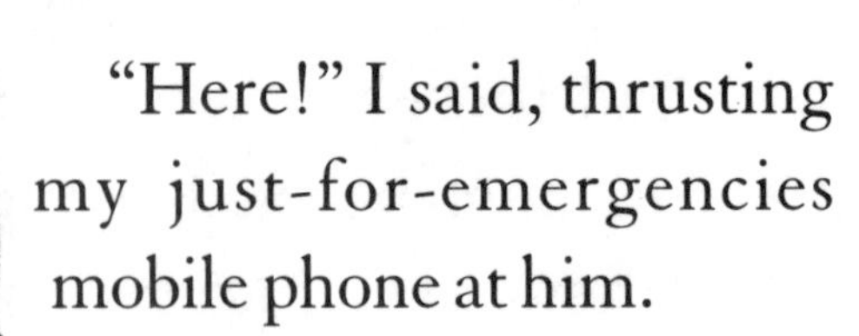

"Here!" I said, thrusting my just-for-emergencies mobile phone at him.

I'd already pressed the short-cut number that immediately dialled through to Mum.

"Um, hello… Is that Mrs Kidd?" Mr Ioannou said warily into the phone.

"Um, yes?" my mum would be saying just as warily at the other end, since I hadn't told her about the **Truly Fantastic Thing** either.

But how could Mr Ioannou and Mum resist such an ace money-making, publicity-grabbing idea?

Wow, this felt exciting.

Right now, I wanted to rush to the craft table in my class and make myself my very own "**You Did Well!**" certificate…

9

The protective socks

Carlsberg the chinchilla was blissfully blissed out with happiness.

The reason? He was being stroked under the chin by Dylan.

Dylan looked pretty blissed out too.

"Hey – is that parrot coming?" asked Caitlin, stomping into the kitchen wearing her new biker boots.

"It's not a parrot, it's a chinchilla," said Dylan.

Caitlin rolled her eyes to the ceiling, then fixed her gaze on me, eyebrows raised.

"Yes, Mum's bringing Ed," I told her. "She thinks it'll help make him less shy and more sociable."

It was Saturday morning, the day of the Fair, and we had to be at school in fifteen minutes to help set up the Petting Zoo.

We were meeting Mum there; she'd be coming directly from the Rescue Centre.

In her van would be: Nightingale the goat, a sheep called Eric, Charlie and Lola the lop-eared rabbits, four guinea pigs whose names I couldn't remember, an iguana called Snoopy and Ed the parrot.

From home (thanks to a lift from Dad) I was bringing Dibbles, Kenneth and George. And Carlsberg, of course. We'd just have to hope he wouldn't be feeling too nocturnal.

Also squashed in the car would be Dylan. Even though he didn't go to my school, Dylan was going to be a Petting Zoo helper. So was Caitlin. At least she was till she realized Ed was coming.

"What's all that about?" asked Dad, as Caitlin turned on her heels and **stomped** back to her room. He was uncomfortably perched on the edge of one of the chairs dotted round the kitchen table. Dad always looks uncomfortable when he's in my house, even though it used to be his house too.

"Ed the parrot really likes Caitlin, but she doesn't much like him," I explained.

Hmm, a bit like me and the trampoline! Only I'd had my leg eaten and she'd had her head clawed. (Ed had clung on super-tight when Mum and I tried to de-tangle him from Caitlin's hair the other day. She said it had felt like having her head stapled.)

"We are going to have to leave quite soon," said Dad, checking his watch, and probably wondering if Caitlin planned to come at all, now that loud rock music was **booming** from her room.

Dad is always checking his watch on Saturdays, as it's his busiest day – usually.

Lucky for me that a wedding had been cancelled that morning (not so lucky for the groom, whose bride had changed her mind), which meant Dad could hang around for a while at the Fair, before the first of his two afternoon weddings.

"Dylan, you'd better lock Carlsberg in now," I told my step-brother, knowing it would take a few minutes to make the chinchilla's cage escape-proof with padlocks and gaffer tape.

After watching him for a few days at home, Mum had decided that Carlsberg was a hyper-intelligent animal who only tried to get free from his cage 'cause he was bored. She said he needed a bigger, stronger cage with lots more toys to stimulate him. But since there was only about fifty pence left in the Rescue Centre bank account now that the rewiring work had started, there wasn't much chance of that happening anytime soon.

"**OK - ready!**" announced Dylan, standing back from the cage – and then frowning when he realized he'd gaffer-taped the cord of his hoodie top to the cage door.

"**OK - ready!**" announced Caitlin, coming back into the kitchen, wearing a sort of slouchy, soft, purple wool cap gone wrong.

I mean, the style of it should have been slouchy; she normally wore it flopping to one side, which looked very cool.

But now ... it looked **mad**.

"Caitlin... Have you got something in there?" I asked.

(Out of the corner of my eye, I could see Dylan struggling to free himself, watched by three dogs and a curious chinchilla.)

"Most of my sock drawer," Caitlin explained, reaching up to pat the hat. "It's to protect my head from claws."

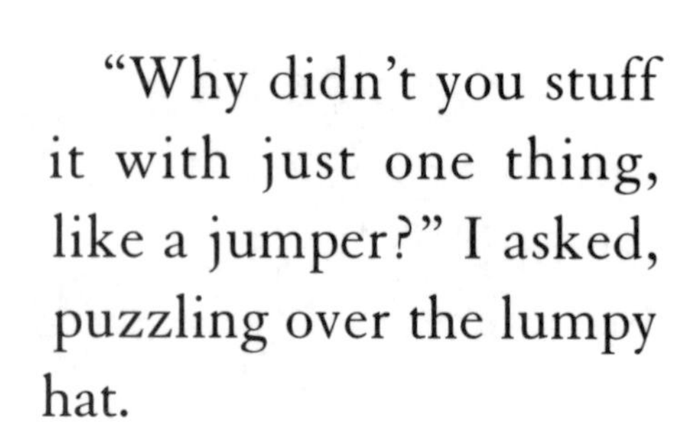

"Why didn't you stuff it with just one thing, like a jumper?" I asked, puzzling over the lumpy hat.

"I tried that, but the socks give it a more natural shape," Caitlin replied casually, as if she was making perfect sense.

I stared at the hat some more, thinking it was the least natural shape I'd ever seen. It looked as if she was hiding a **knobbly** alien head under there. Or maybe a litter of snoozing kittens or something.

"Well, let's get going," said Dad, gazing warily at Caitlin's head. "There're a lot of us to pack in the car, and it'll take a bit of organizing now that we've got to squeeze Caitlin's hat in too..."

Hurrah! We were on our way (er, once we'd found the scissors and cut Dylan's hoodie cord free).

Today was going to be just the best fun, and do lots of good for the school and the Rescue Centre, I was sure.

Yep, I wasn't going to whinge or moan about anything being unfair any more, 'cause today, everything was going to be amazingly, unstoppably great.

wasn't it...?

I win!! And it's so unfair...

"Squeeeeet!"

"Now if you could just not hold him quite so tightly..." I said to the small girl trying lovingly to crush Lettuce the guinea pig.

"But he is soooooo cute!!" said the four-year-old, her fingers in a vice-like grip around Lettuce's chest.

"Yes, he is," I replied, gently but firmly peeling her fingers away.

I was thinking that Lettuce wouldn't be quite so cute if he was dead.

"**AW**...**!**" groaned the girl, realizing that her time was up. "Can't I have another hug?"

"You'll have to give more money to the girl at the gate!" I said, pointing to Soph, who was at the entrance of the *Paws For Thought* "enclosure".

Our Petting Zoo was a huge hit at the School Fair. There was a snaking queue of people waiting to get in, armed with their fifty pences.

And for fifty pence, you could:

a) come in and coo at the animals,

b) cuddle a rabbit, guinea pig or iguana, and...

c) stroke a goat, sheep, or dog or three.

Being a bit more of a wild animal than, say, Dibbles, Carlsberg the chinchilla wasn't going to be allowed out to be stroked or cuddled. But for fifty pence, you could have a go at renaming him. (Dylan was looking after this bit, taking money and writing down suggestions very slowly on a clipboard, with his tongue poking out of the corner of his mouth.)

"Here you go!" announced Dad, handing Soph a cold drink first, and struggling into the enclosure balancing an armful of cardboard cups for the rest of us.

"Thanks, Dad," I said, taking a cup from him as the bunny squasher sulkily turned to go.

"And one for you, Lynne," said Dad, handing a drink to Mum. "And there you are, Caitlin, and Dylan... You know, I don't have to leave for my wedding for another fifteen minutes. If any of you want to go and have a look around the rest of the Fair, I can help out here!"

"Yes – if you or Dylan or Soph want to go off for a quick wander, that's absolutely fine!" Mum added, glancing up from Eric the sheep and Nightingale the goat, who were frantically nibbling seedy treats from the hands of giggling little kids.

Ed the parrot clung on to her shoulder, shyly peeking at me, as if he was waiting for an answer, same as Mum.

"Um... I don't really want to, though," I replied with a shrug.

"Me neither!" Soph called out over her shoulder.

"Me neither too!" Dylan joined in.

We were all having way too good a time here with the animals to care that much about the Hook-a-Duck and the home-made cake stalls.

"Fair enough," said Dad with a shrug, stepping aside as the next flurry of kids and grown-up came in to **ooh** and **aah** at the animal "But hey, listen – I've had another ide about how you can make more money for the school..."

"Oh, yeah?"

I gazed up at Dad, as I put poor, squished Lettuce back in his cage for a rest. Instead, I brought out Apple, Carrot and Celery the guine pigs for the three smiling little boys no standing waiting for their turn.

"Yeah, I thought maybe you could have a 'Guess What's Under Caitlin's Hat!' competition. The winner could have Caitlin come round to their house, and she'd play their favourite tune on her didgeridoo!"

I sniggered so much at Dad's suggestion that I made the guinea pigs jiggle.

Caitlin – who was looking after Snoopy the iguana as well as our dogs – gave Dad a withering look, and shook her head at him.

That got me and Dad both sniggering even more, since it made her weird hat wobble.

"Indie?"

I spun round to see who was talking.

It was my teacher, Miss Levy. She had a big smile on her face and a hot dog in her hand.

"This is **fantastic**, Indie!" she said, looking around at our busy Petting Zoo. "The queue for this is longer than the one for face-painting and for the bouncy slide!"

Miss Levy looked different out of school – she was wearing jeans and a floaty, long-sleeved top, with pretty sparkly thread at the edges. She didn't look quite like my Miss Levy.

"Thanks!" I muttered shyly.

It's funny how you can feel shy when you see your teacher outside of the classroom, isn't it? But hey, maybe I'm just a bit stupid.

"This is my mum and my dad," I said, pointing to Mum (with the parrot stuck to her shoulder) and Dad (who put out his hand to try to shake Miss Levy's, only hers was holding a hot dog).

And it was pretty silly of me to introduce Miss Levy, since she already knew Mum and Dad from parents' evenings and everything.

Duh!

"Hi there!" Miss Levy smiled at them both, swapping her hot dog round so she could shake Dad's hand. "And I hope you'll be getting lots of publicity from this, Mrs Kidd – I've just seen Fee handing out leaflets about the Rescue Centre, left, right and centre!"

"And here comes some more publicity!" said Dad, reaching into his bag and pulling out his camera. "Miss Levy ... Indie ... Lynne... Can you all squeeze together, so I can get a shot of you? I'll send it to the News Desk of the newspaper I work for. It'll be in next week's paper!"

We squeezed, along with the three guinea pigs I was still holding, Ed the parrot (of course), and Nightingale the goat. It felt a bit funny, to be squashed right up against my teacher – as weird as the idea of Dad turning up at school to teach our class. She smelled nice, though, close up. All flowery perfume and hot dog.

"Ready?" said Dad. "Here we go!"

Then three sounds happened at exactly the same time.

The "**Ooh!**" came from Miss Levy, as Nightingale stretched out her neck and pinched the hot dog from her hand – as well as tearing a bite-sized chunk out of the sleeve of her pretty, floaty top.

The **gulp!** was the hot dog – and chunk of sleeve – being swallowed whole.

The **snap!** was Dad capturing it all on camera.

The next sound was a tinkle, as Dad reached into his pocket for a handful of coins.

"Oops! Let me get you another one of those," he said – meaning a hot dog and not a top, I think.

"I'm so sorry!" Mum apologized, hauling Nightingale away, chomping happily with a trail of sparkly thread hanging out of her mouth.

"Don't worry! It was an old top! It's fine, honestly!!" said Miss Levy, but in that sort of way that makes you unsure if she really meant it was fine or not.

Eek!

Can teachers sack you from their class for stuff like that...?

Three hours and ten minutes after the hot-dog-and-sleeve vanishing act, my cheeks were – I hoped – getting back to normal after flushing bright pink earlier.

Still, I hadn't had too much time to think about the shame of it all. The queue for the Petting Zoo had only just faded to a trickle.

"Ah, this is lovely, Indie!" Mrs O'Neill sighed happily, leaning over the Petting Zoo fence for a chat.

She'd wandered over from the gym (i.e. the School Fair café) where she'd treated herself to two ice-creams in a row.

That was to celebrate her luck on the tombola; she seemed very chuffed with her voucher for an eyebrow-shaping session at the local beauty salon.

"Have you been on the bouncy slide, yet, Indie? If I were half my age, I'd be tempted to give it a go!" she chortled.

"I haven't – I've been busy here all afternoon, Mrs O'Neill," I said, pointing my thumb behind me towards our animal gang.

"Too busy? But you youngsters are missing all the **fun!**" gasped Mrs O'Neill. "There's a raffle and everything!"

I didn't say so, but I knew I wasn't missing much with the raffle: it was full of pants prizes like, er, pants (fancy frilly ones from the ladies' undies shop in the High Street), a bottle of sherry (I don't think so!) and a bunch of "Just For Men" toiletries (just not worth bothering with).

And who could forget the nuttiest prize of all? **Get this** – Miss Levy had put herself in the raffle as a prize! Not a take-home-for-ever kind of a prize: she'd offered to come round and read a kid a bedtime story, in their own home.

(How fantastic if you were in the Nursery or Reception class. How **mortifying** if you were over six.)

Miss Levy had told Dad all about it when they'd gone to get her another hot dog. She'd also told Dad that she hoped I wasn't all embarrassed about what Nightingale had done. Dad said I'd get over it, which was a big, fat lie. I didn't know how I could face Miss Levy on Monday morning at school. My stomach was already tied in knots at the very idea.

"Actually, Mrs O'Neill, would you like to come in and have a go at renaming our chinchilla?" I asked, trying to take my mind off the shame stuff.

"Ooh, yes, please!" said Mrs O'Neill, as I waved her into the Petting Zoo enclosure. "Er, remind me, Indie... What is a chin—?"

"Where do I pay?" a voice suddenly interrupted.

The interrupting voice belonged to Simon Green. **Great.**

"Right there – see Soph," I said, pointing to Soph, and the sign beside her that read "Entry: 50p".

"How much is it to get in?" demanded Simon Stupid Green.

"Fifty pence," I told him, wearily.

"Only got thirty. Will that do?"

"No!" I said firmly.

"Oh, let the lad in, Indie!" Mrs O'Neill smiled beseechingly at me. "After all, the Fair's nearly over!"

I guessed she was right about the Fair being nearly over. I could hear Mr Ioannou now on a microphone on the just-out-of-sight stage. He was thanking everyone for coming, and getting ready to announce the winners of the raffle.

"**Great!**" said Simon Green, chucking a twenty-pence piece at Soph and hurrying through.

He made a beeline for Carlsberg. I felt responsible for both the chinchilla and Dylan – since Simon Green is such a germ – but Mrs O'Neill seemed to be suddenly demanding a guided tour of the animals.

"Heavens! What's that?" she asked, pointing at Snoopy, who Caitlin was just about to put back in his cage.

"An iguana," I explained.

"An ig-whattie?" Mrs O'Neill mumbled.

Caitlin winked at me. She was having a great time, and she hadn't had a flicker of perch-like interest from Ed the parrot. For the whole afternoon he'd sat rigidly on Mum's shoulder, with his head pulled so low down into his body with shyness that his beak and startled eyes only just peeked over the top of his feathery, puffball body.

"It's a sort of lizard," I said, taking Snoopy very gently from Caitlin, so that Mrs O'Neill could take a closer look.

"AND THE WINNER OF THESE RATHER... ER... I MEAN, THIS, UM, COLOURFUL UNDERWEAR..." Mr Ioannou's voice boomed uncertainly from the speakers. "...IS RAFFLE TICKET NUMBER–"

"Ooh, let me get my tickets!" said Mrs O'Neill, scrabbling about in her handbag.

Snoopy the iguana blinked at her. Like me, he was probably trying to imagine Mrs O'Neill wearing pink-edged turquoise bikini briefs.

Hmmm...

"Indie! He won't stop it!!" I suddenly heard Dylan yelp.

I spun round quickly, to see what was wrong. Caitlin did the same.

My spin made me feel strangely *queasy.*

Caitlin's spin sent her stuffed hat flying off her head.

"What's all that?" asked Mrs O'Neill, staring at the scattering of socks raining down onto the ground.

FOOD! thought Nightingale the goat, straining on the lead that Mum had her tethered with.

But so what if the socks had turned into an instant goat snack? Dylan needed help:

Simon The Germ Green was trying to open Carlsberg the chinchilla's cage!!

"AND THE WINNER OF THIS FANTASTIC TOILETRIES SET IS..." Mr Ioannou's voice boomed out some more in the background.

"This boy has suggested a very rude new name for Carlsberg!" Dylan said in a panicked voice, trying to put himself in between Carlsberg's cage and Simon Green. "And he only gave me seven pence for his suggestion!"

"So? That money means I should get to play with this thing!" Simon insisted.

No it didn't. I leapt across Nightingale's back, aiming somehow to rugby-tackle the Human Germ before he got the cage open. But something got there before me; something shy, plump, feathery and protective.

"AAAHHHH!" yelped Simon Green, as a pair of claws dug deep into his head.

He stumbled back, fell over Nightingale, and landed with his head thumping down onto Mrs O'Neill's neat grey lace-ups.

"What's going on?" Mum suddenly asked, lunging over Simon Green, as Ed flup-flup-flupped his way back to the safety of her shoulder.

Wow – he wasn't so much of a dodo as a guard-dog. A guard-parrot?

"This lad was trying to get that fluffy hamster thing out of its cage!" said Mrs O'Neill, frowning down at Simon Green and trying to shake his head off her shoes. "Young Dylan was trying to stop him!"

"Get off my socks!" Caitlin's order was aimed at Nightingale, who was still trying to chomp on the socks currently buried under Simon Green. Of course Simon didn't know that, and thought that Caitlin was just one more person glowering down at him.

From his viewpoint on the ground, he stared round at a growing circle of scowling faces that included me, Mum, Mrs O'Neill, Caitlin, Soph, Fee, Dylan and Ed.

Then Nightingale started head-butting him in the side to get at a particularly tasty-looking stripy sock.

"Leave me alone!!" yelped Simon Green, scrambling to his feet and hurrying out of the Petting Zoo.

"Bye! We'll miss you!!" giggled Fee, wiggling her fingers at his retreating back.

At that point, my mobile phone rang. In a fug of confusion, I lifted an iguana to my ear and said, "Hello?"

One nano-second later, I swapped Snoopy for the phone in my back pocket.

"Hello?"

"Indie! Can't speak – I've got to photograph a bride on a unicycle in a second," Dad's voice chattered. "But just wanted to remind you that I left all my raffle tickets with you. Can you listen out in case any of my numbers are called? There's a particular something I hope I win – and I think you can guess why! Sorry – **whoooahh!** Here she comes; got to go!"

A bride on a unicycle?! Dad was seriously the weirdest wedding photographer in the world, I decided, as I grabbed the wodge of tickets from my jeans pocket and flicked through them.

They ran from number 070 to number 150. (Yes, I'd bullied him into buying lots once I got my replacements from the school office!)

And what was he on about with the raffle prizes? What did he want to win? And why did he think I would be able to guess why?

"AND THE WINNER OF OUR FINAL RAFFLE PRIZE – HAVING A PERSONAL BEDTIME STORY READ TO YOU TOMORROW NIGHT BY OUR VERY OWN MISS LEVY! – IS TICKET NUMBER ... 071!"

Uh-oh.

That was one of **Dad's tickets!**

But what would he do with a prize like that? I didn't think Fiona my step-mum would much like Miss Levy sitting at the edge of their bed reading Dad *The Gruffalo*.

Uh-oh, uh-oh, uh-oh...

Dad wanted the prize for *me*. He'd wanted to win, to get me and Miss Levy together, after today's mega-embarrassment!

Blah – my stomach tied itself in a grumbly double knot at the very (shameful) idea.

Would anyone notice if I fed a winning raffle ticket to a greedy goat...?

The bedtime reading blues

It was Sunday night.

It was 8 p.m.

It was twenty-eight hours and five minutes since I'd found out that Dad's raffle ticket had won the "super" prize of the bedtime story from Miss Levy.

Sure enough, he'd given the prize to me. ("Won't it be great, Indie!" he'd said on the phone the night before.

"Having your very own teacher all to yourself? You two will have such a laugh!" **Er,** no we wouldn't.)

So tonight was the night she'd be coming to read to me. My stomach was now in a mega-knot, with extra added rumbling and grumbling thrown in.

I had to do something to take my mind off it. I couldn't just sit there casually on my bed in my leggings and T-shirt (no way was I going to be in pyjamas!), all a-flutter with dread.

So I started jumping on the bed.

BOING!!

Got to find something else to think about, I told myself.

BOING!!

Bum.

BOING!!

I didn't mean to be rude – I'd just remembered that *that* was the new name Simon Green had come up with for Carlsberg.

BOING!!

Not that Mum and I would be choosing it!

BOING!!

Actually, Mum and I thought we'd probably end up going for one of Dylan's suggestions, since he'd entered the competition thirty-two times yesterday afternoon.

BOING!!

He must have just re-watched all of the *Lord of the Rings* trilogy with Dad and Fiona, 'cause every suggestion was a name of a character from the films.

BOING!!

Gorbag, Shagrat and Legolas didn't really seem to suit a dippy chinchilla, but we quite liked Frodo.

BOING!!

Or did that sound more like the sort of name that would suit a frog?

BOING!

"Oh!" said Mum, opening the bedroom door all of a sudden.

BOING-de-doinggggg... went the springs of the bed as I quickly tried to bounce myself to a standstill.

"I did knock!" said Mum, as she, Dad

and Miss Levy stood in the doorway, staring in.

"I think I was maybe ... y'know... boinging too loudly to hear..." I mumbled, quickly sitting cross-legged on my bed.

"Just getting some practice in for the new school trampoline?" asked Miss Levy, coming into the room.

OK, so she'd made a bit of a joke, but I didn't feel like laughing. Between the sleeve-'n'-hot-dog-munching moment and that weird awkwardness of seeing my teacher out of school, I felt a little like throwing up.

And it was about to get **worse.**

"Hope you don't mind that I came along, Indie – but I thought it would be great to get a picture of this special occasion!" Dad said, slipping into professional photographer mode. "Now Miss Levy, if you could sit on the left-hand side of the bed, and hold the book open, with the cover up, so I can see it..."

"Ahem," Miss Levy coughed, doing as she was told, same as I did what I was told when she spoke in class. "Like this?"

"Great!" said Dad, as Miss Levy showed off the cover of the Harry Potter book she'd brought along.

Click, click!

"Fantastic! Can you just pretend to be reading now, Miss Levy?" Dad instructed, moving in for a close-up. Dibbles had suddenly padded in and flopped his head on the duvet, trying to figure out what was going on, and whether it involved food.

"Hope you don't mind my choosing this," Miss Levy said, looking at me sideways. "I was pretty sure I remembered you saying you liked Harry Potter."

"Mmmm," I mumbled.

I did like Harry Potter, but I didn't much like the way the knots in my stomach were getting tighter, then loose and floppy, then tighter again...

"And if both of you could give me sort of half-smiles?" Dad asked, his face hidden behind his camera.

"Yewwwwww..." Miss Levy groaned instead.

"Sorry!" said Mum, smelling the same sudden iffy smell. "Dibbles! Out!! Now!!"

As Mum shooed our windy dog out of the room, I suddenly felt sick:

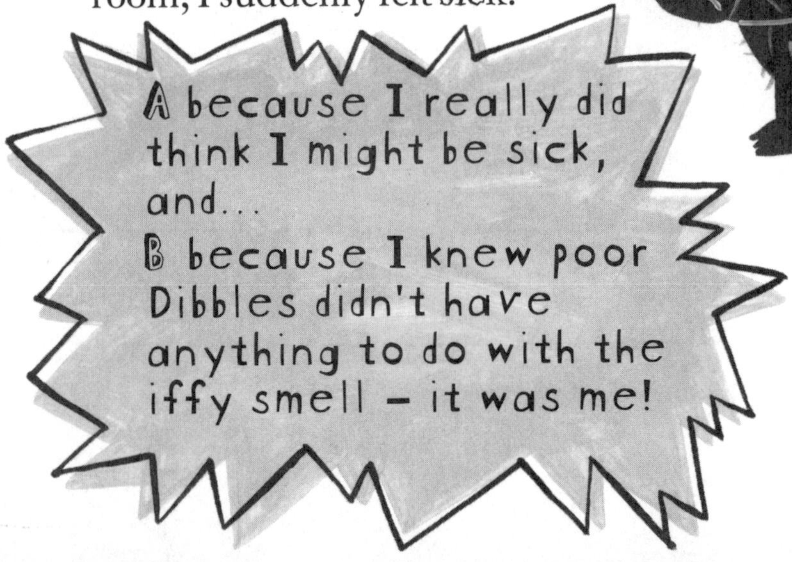

A because I really did think I might be sick, and...

B because I knew poor Dibbles didn't have anything to do with the iffy smell – it was me!

Oh, the shame...

"Indie, are you all right?" asked Dad, lowering his camera. "You look a bit, well, green!"

"Ah, I think Indie might have the tummy bug that's been going around school," said Miss Levy, putting a hand on my (green) forehead.

"What is it?" asked Mum, hurtling back into the room.

"**Urgh**..." was all I managed to mumble, as my insides started to do backward flips and star jumps. (Sounds exciting, but felt awful.)

Mr Ioannou had gone on about the symptoms during an assembly, hadn't he? Now I wished I'd listened, instead of thinking my knotty, gurgly tummy was just down to nerves and humiliation.

"There's been a lot of sickness and diarrhoea at school!" Miss Levy explained for Mum's benefit. "Think we might need to get Indie to the bathroom..."

Mum and Miss Levy took an elbow each and lifted me up off the bed.

"Here – take this, just in case," said Dad, giving my Spongebob Squarepants bin to Mum, as a look-alike sick-bag, I guess.

Well, Dad might have hoped that Miss Levy and I would have bonded over our bedtime reading, but now I felt more embarrassed than ever in front of her.

At least he'd helped out with the bin, which I might well have to use in the next five seconds, the way my tummy was gurgling.

And it would come in handy in class: I could wear it over my head, so I'd never have to look Miss Levy in the eye ever again...

12 You Did Well!

"Hey, kid – let's read your horoscope," said Caitlin, sticking her feet up on my bed.

She was wearing her new, clompy biker boots, but I didn't care, 'cause …

(A) I felt too yucky, and

(B) my bed was messy enough with old tissues, two dogs (Dibbles and Kenneth), a book I'd got bored of reading and a half-chewed dog toy George had left there.

"It says, 'You will have an exciting week out and about, with lots going on'," Caitlin read out with a frown.

Ha! It was Monday morning and the doctor had told Mum that I'd probably have to stay off school all week, till I stopped feeling *yucky*.

"Don't think I believe in horoscopes," I mumbled, from under my duvet.

"Me neither," said Caitlin, throwing the magazine over her shoulder with a flutter. "So what do you want to do now?"

"Nothing," I said glumly, wishing I was un-*yucky* and hanging out with Soph and Fee at school, hearing all the gossip about Saturday's School Fair – though school would be out now, I realized, glancing at the pink clock on my bedside table.

Still, I was quite glad to have missed out on seeing Miss Levy, after the total blah-ness of yesterday evening...

BING-BONG!!

"MEE-HOOOOWLL!!"

yelped Kenneth, as Dibbles **thudded** off the bed and tried to squash himself underneath, to hide from the noise.

"I'll get it!" said Caitlin, taking her boots off the bed and clomping off down the stairs – accompanied by Kenneth – to see who was at the door.

Poor Caitlin; she'd spent the whole day trying to cheer me up and keep me entertained. She'd played a ton of new tunes on her didgeridoo.

She'd shown me cool celeb sites online. She'd played Monopoly with me, till Dibbles ran off with the dice.

She'd even told me the whole plot line of her favourite horror movie, with lot of actions thrown in.

She must be exhausted, and already ticking off the days till I went back to school...

stomp, stomp, stomp.

Actually, that was an awful lot of stomping on the stairs!

I quickly ran my hand over my hair to make sure it wasn't sticking up in a stupid point or something, and got ready for whoever my visitors were.

said Fee, breezing into the room, followed by Soph. "So you've had a case of the collywobbles!"

"Huh? But that means nerves!" I answered her, showing I knew what her big words meant.

"Yeah, but it can also mean dodgy tummy stuff too!" she giggled, being funny and frighteningly knowledgeable at the same time.

"So, how are you, Indie?" asked Soph.

"A bit better. But you shouldn't come too close – you might get my bug," I warned them both.

"OK – we'll stay down this end of your bed," said Soph, emptying a plastic bag out on the duvet. "Here!"

She'd just showered me with magazines, plus a **ginormous** bag of M&Ms (I'd have to keep that till I felt better.)

"Oh, and here's a 'Get Well Soon' card from Miss Levy," added Fee, handing me a pink envelope.

"How did the bedtime reading thing go last night?" asked Soph. She and Fee both knew how much I'd been dreading it, especially after seeing what Nightingale had done.

"Terrible. Horrible. That's when I suddenly started to feel ill," I explained, as I tore the envelope open.

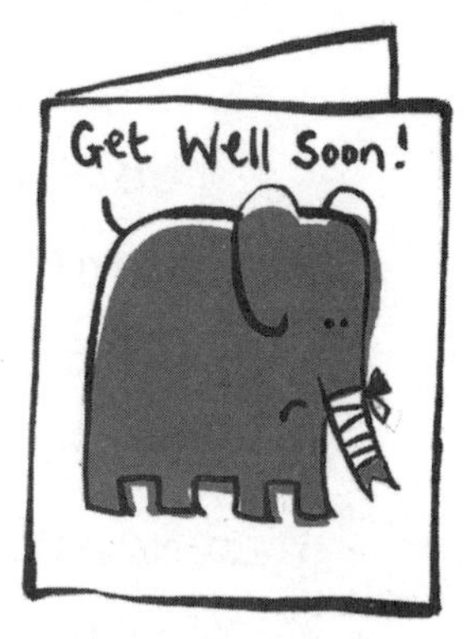

Ah, cute! The card had a drawing of an elephant with its trunk bandaged. And I couldn't help smiling at the message inside:

"Well, Indie – I didn't know you wanted to get out of my bedtime book-reading session THAT badly! Hope you feel better soon, Miss Levy x

PS Hope the goat didn't get indigestion from eating my shirt!"

Hee hee... Miss Levy really was *so* nice. Maybe I wouldn't need to wear my Spongebob Squarepants bin on my head when I went back to school *after* all.

"And we've got some **MORE** school news!" Soph beamed, opening my M&Ms and helping herself.

"Yep!" Fee joined in. "At assembly, Mr Ioannou said the School Fair had been a **HUGE** success, and that the Petting Zoo had raised the most money of all the attractions!"

"Really?" I said, a ripple of happiness wriggling across my chest. (Which felt a lot nicer than the tummy star-jumps I'd been suffering from yesterday.)

"Really!" Soph nodded. "And he said that SO much money was raised, the school can have lots of new gym stuff, with money left over. So he's going to donate the rest to the Rescue Centre!!"

Wow!

It looked as if the cats in the cat block could stop eating their tea by candlelight sooner than Mum expected.

And Carlsberg/Frodo the chinchilla could be in his super-strong cage-cum-entertainment-centre pretty soon too!

"Mr Ioannou even had a surprise for you," Fee said with a smile. "He called you up to the stage to give you one of his "**You Did Well!**" certificates – but Miss Levy had to tell him you were off sick."

"**AW!**" I groaned, aching with disappointment. "But I've always wanted to go up on stage and get a certificate from Mr Ioannou!"

"Yeah, but with your luck at the moment, you'd probably have tripped and fallen flat on your face or something," Fee wisely pointed out.

"Mmm, maybe," I mumbled, thinking how bad it would have been to go splat in front of the whole school.

"But even though you weren't there, everyone cheered and clapped for you anyway!" Soph babbled on. "Well, everyone except for Simon Green, who booed, but he is a great big noodle, remember."

But I didn't care about Simon Green and his dumb old booing, 'cause Soph was just handing me my very own "You Did Well!" certificate!

I **LOVED** it, even if it did have a weird orange splodge on it...

"Sorry – spaghetti bolognese for school dinners today!" she shrugged.

"Never mind!" I said, quickly kneeling my way over the bed to give my two best mates a happiness hug.

"Er, I know friends are meant to share stuff," I heard Fee suddenly mumble in my ear, "but I'd rather not share your bugs, Indie..."

Mmm – that gave me an idea. Maybe I should go back to school tomorrow, and give Simon Green a great, big, squishy hug.

Not because I'm a lovely, kind, forgiving girl, but because he's a boy who definitely deserves a case of the collywobbles!

"Three cheers for Indie!" yelped Soph, as I unhugged my friends. "Hurray!"

"Hurray!" Fee joined in noisily.

"Hurray!" Caitlin hollered along, appearing at the bedroom door with a tray of drinks for us.

"MEE-HOOOOOWLL!!" howled Kenneth, who didn't have a clue what was going on, but was quite excited anyway.

And speaking of excited, I needed to call Mum and tell her the good news.

But maybe – funny tummy or not – I might try just ONE teeny weeny M&M to celebrate.

Well, that was only fair, wasn't it...?!